I0767068

Introducing Miss Emelina Hewitt and Stanley in ...

No Clues No Shoes

Written by
Marsha Casper Cook

Illustrated by
Paisley Hansen

Published by
MICHIGAN
AVENUE
MEDIA
LLC

Acknowledgments

I would like to thank my two editors, Marcus Cook and Jeff Fleischer for all their hard work. Without them I would be lost.

And to Robin from Fideli Publishing I sincerely appreciate everything she has done for me, and the endless hours of conversations that have made all the difference in the world to me. I have learned so much and I most definitely owe all my newfound knowledge to her. Again, thanks for everything…

To Paisley thank you for bringing Emelina to life, because without you she might still be in the piles of things to do.

And to Stephen thank you for listening or pretending to be listening. You let me be the free spirit that Emelina is!

Thank you Mary Rita, Pat and Vicki R, from Julia Philips Literary Agency.

A special thank you goes to Bonnie — if it wasn't for her I might never have ever tried.

And to all those kids out there who think about writing and wonder if they have what it takes … don't give up. I never did!

CHAPTER ONE

My name is Emelina Hewitt, and I am eight years old. I have the greatest best friend in the whole world. His name is Addison Jamison Apple, but I call him AJ. He doesn't look like an apple. Then again … maybe he does. Just kidding. I'll tell you about our first adventure, but first let me tell you how we met. It's just like my grandmother always said, "First things first."

Before we begin, it's very important that you understand a few things about me. I like to talk. Sometimes I talk too much. I ask a lot of questions because I think that's how you learn different things. When I start to go on and on my dog, Stanley, starts to sing. "Do re mi fa so la ti do." That's how I know when to stop. Stanley sings and I stop talking. However, there are those times when I have been known to keep right on going. Like right now. Uh oh, there he goes …

AJ and his family moved into our neighborhood in the summer but, because we weren't in school yet, we had never met. I did see him at the park with his dog while I was jogging with Stanley. Stanley doesn't like to jog, but he's such a good sport that he does it because he knows I love jogging. He thinks watching TV and clicking the remote is exercise.

One day, before dinner, we decided to take a walk down the street where AJ lived.I thought AJ could use a new friend. He probably left all his friends behind when his family moved. There he was, sitting on his porch. I could hardly see his eyes because his hat covered them up. He was reading a book and didn't seem to notice us, but he was eating popcorn and it really smelled great. Even though I didn't like to eat between meals, I decided to make an exception.

"Hi," I called out to him, trying to get his attention. "I hate to interrupt you, but I saw you the other day at the park with your dog and I haven't seen you since. I live down the street. My name is Emelina Hewitt, and this is my dog Stanley."

He finally looked up, and then I knew why he had his eyes covered. He might have been crying or something like that. He looked at me for few seconds and finally said, "Hi, my name is AJ Apple and my dog's name was Sammy."

"Was? What happened? Is he sick? Did he get hurt?" I curiously asked.

AJ seemed a little annoyed. "Do you always ask so many questions?"

"Yes, as a matter of fact I do," I said, a little annoyed at his question.

We stared at each other for a few minutes and then AJ said, "If you don't ask me any more questions, you can stay."

This meeting wasn't going as planned, but the popcorn smelled good. So I decided to stay. I wondered what happened to his dog, but a promise is a promise. It was difficult for me to just sit there, but I did. I really wanted some popcorn, but I promised not to ask a question. "Can I have some popcorn?" was a question. I thought for a moment and then said, "Boy, that popcorn smells good."

"Do you want some?" AJ asked as he leaned toward me, still reading his book. I wondered how he did that. If I did that, the popcorn would probably be scattered all over the porch. AJ began reading his book out loud. Stanley seemed to enjoy AJ reading to him. I would have rather had a conversation, but that was not going to happen.

CHAPTER TWO

A few days later, I started Private Detective School. Guess who was sitting right next to me? It was AJ. You can imagine how surprised I was to see him there, and he was very surprised to see me. He sat at a desk next to me and Stanley sat between us.

The first few days of Private Detective School were pretty easy because our teacher, Detective Duke Dachshund the Third, didn't think we were ready to be detectives. Finally, after talking and talking and more talking, I convinced our teacher we were ready to learn how to solve crimes. So we started our training, and AJ and I were at the top of our class.

I was not surprised, but it seemed like everyone else was, especially Detective Duke Dachshund. Never underestimate a girl with a plan. That was another one of my grandmother's favorite sayings.

During our classes, it seemed like AJ started getting used to me. He didn't seem to mind some of my questions, but he didn't answer them either. Well, there you have it. AJ and I were very different, but we became friends. Soon, we would graduate from Private Detective School. We would both be private detectives and I knew that's when the fun would begin.

It happened just a little bit sooner than I imagined but, like my grandmother always used to say, "You can plan your future but life happens anyway." I'm not quite sure what that means. When I get older, I will not only remember the things my grandmother said, but I will understand them. There goes Stanley singing … "Do re me fa so la ti do."

It was Wednesday, library day. AJ and I were both reading. Well, actually, he was reading and I was sightseeing, which really means not reading but just looking at the pictures. I really love sightseeing.

All of a sudden, a boy in the back of the room shouted out, "Someone has stolen one of my sneakers!" I jumped up and ran to the back of the room, while AJ didn't even seem to hear the boy shout. That's AJ when he concentrates.

"I can help!" I called out as I stood before the boy. "I'm Emelina Hewitt. I'm a private detective. My motto is, 'If it's out there I can find it. Have you ever heard of me?'"

"Nope," he answered. "Never have."

"You will," I answered back. I reached into my pocket and pulled out a notepad. I remembered my grandmother's words. First things first. "So, what's your name?"

"My name is Frankie Finkel and my mother is going to be very mad at me if I don't find my shoe. I just got them yesterday. Can you help?"

"I know how it is," I said to him. "I lost a pair of shoes one day and, boy, was my mom mad. I didn't find them and, well, that night I didn't get to watch TV or anything…"

Suddenly, Stanley appeared singing. "Do re mi…" Uh oh, he was right. I needed to do my job and stop talking.

I was on my way back to tell AJ what had happened when Miss Bookmark, the librarian, tapped me on the shoulder. "I certainly hope you can solve our problem," she whispered in my ear.

Science Fiction
Fantasy
Historical
SUMMER READING LIST
The Adventures of Tom Sawyer
by Mark Twain
The Scarlet Letter
by Nathaniel Hawthorne
Ms. Bookmark

"Our problem? What exactly do you mean by that, Miss Bookmark?"

"This isn't the first sneaker that's disappeared this week."

"Aha," I said as I continued to write in my notepad. It's a good thing I watched a lot of TV shows and I listened to everything Detective Duke Dachshund said at Private Detective School, because I was ready to take on this case.

So, with pride, I put my hands on my hips and looked at Miss Bookmark with all the confidence in the world. "Have no fear, Emelina Hewitt is here," I said. And then I flexed my muscles and walked away. I was so busy flexing my muscles, I didn't realize AJ was right behind me.

He didn't look happy. "Did I hear you say we're going to take a case?" he asked.

"You most certainly did," I said, feeling pretty good about my decision.

"But we haven't finished school yet," AJ said. "We're not ready to take a case."

"We're almost finished with Detective School. Someone took a boy named Frankie Finkel's sneaker. All we have to do is find it. How hard can that be?"

"We don't have enough experience. In fact, we don't have any experience," AJ said as he reached into his pocket and took out a candy bar. "Want some?" he asked.

"No thanks, not right now. I have to finish my notes. How can you eat at a time like this? It's our very first case. Aren't you excited?"

"Aren't you even a little bit scared?" AJ asked while still munching on his candy bar.

"No way, we can do this. Have a little faith," I answered back. I wasn't scared. In fact, I never even thought about being scared until AJ brought it up. Well, I might have been a little scared, but I wasn't about to tell him.

CHAPTER THREE

AJ and I began to search the library for clues. When we finished, we were clueless. No clues, no shoes. It was then I knew it was going to be a lot harder than I thought.

Then the idea of the century came to me. Why not check the lost and found? Last year, I lost five pairs of gloves, three scarves, four pens, two pairs of sunglasses, four hats, and two notebooks. This year, I was much more responsible and hadn't lost a thing. Of course, school just started a few weeks earlier.

So there we were at the lost and found. It was quite a big box, a lot bigger than last year. I reached inside and pulled out a couple of socks. Let me tell you, they were really smelly. I had to hold my breath after I took a whiff.

LOST
&
FOUND

"Your turn," I said to AJ as he waited for me to finish. AJ dug so deep into the box that he almost fell in. "Look what I found," he said as he pulled up a pencil case and a bag of cookies.

"Better throw them back in the box," I said. "Or, better yet, throw them in the garbage. Who wants a bag of stale cookies?"

"They're mine. I lost them on the first day of school," AJ said as he got ready to open the bag of cookies.

"Are you always this hungry?" I asked.

"Yes, as a matter of fact, I am always hungry." AJ was getting annoyed. "Do you have to keep asking so many questions?"

"That's just part of my personality. My grandmother used to say I was a very curious little girl with a gigantic imagination."

I suggested we eat lunch, hoping AJ would stop being so grumpy. The more he ate, the less grumpy he was.

"Okay, I got it," I said. "I won't ask any questions for the rest of the day. How's that?"

"I don't think that will happen," AJ mumbled to himself.

"Me either," Stanley added.

AJ stopped walking. He was stunned. "Emelina, did you hear that?"

"Hear what?" I asked, pretending not to know what he was about to ask.

"Did Stanley just say something?" I wanted to laugh, but I kept a straight face.

"Stanley, talk? No he doesn't talk. I think you've had too much candy. Your brain is candy clogged."

"Candy clogged? What does that mean?" AJ asked.

"It means you need to eat more fruit and you need to stop munching on junk food," I said.

Luckily, AJ was thinking only about lunch, so the question about Stanley was passed over.

CHAPTER FOUR

After lunch, AJ and I started to walk back to school, but AJ seemed a little down in the dumps. AJ began to walk quickly and furiously, like he was in a big hurry.

"Hey, AJ, slow down," I called out. When he didn't stop or even slow down a little, I began to jog faster and faster. It's a good thing I jog every day. Otherwise, Stanley and I wouldn't have been able to keep up with him. We did end up making it back to the playground in record time.

Finally, AJ stopped running. "I'm sorry," he said as he sat down on the grass and wiped the tears from his eyes. "It's about my dog, Sammy. He died a couple of days after we moved here. He was pretty old, and he lived a lot longer than he was supposed to. I really miss him, and I can't seem to

forget him. I don't think I ever will, and I don't know if that's a bad thing."

Stanley kissed AJ's face with lots of wet, sloppy kisses. For the first time since I met him, AJ smiled. He seemed to feel better after that. Maybe he just needed to get it off his chest.

"AJ, I think that remembering someone you love isn't a bad thing. Right before my grandmother died, she gave me a kiss and said, 'Keep the memories of me in your heart. If you ever feel sad and alone, remember the good times we shared and the love I had for you, and you will never be alone.'"

"Does it work for you?" AJ asked.

"Yes, it does," I said as I reached for his hand and pulled him up from the ground. I was a lot stronger than he thought.

"I have an idea," I said to AJ. "It's actually a good idea. We can share Stanley."

"Really?" AJ asked.

"Yes, if that will make you happy," I said.

"Let's get going. We've got a case to finish. And yes, Stanley does talk. Not all the time, just when he feels like it.

He now considers you family. If he didn't, he wouldn't have said anything."

Well, seeing AJ so happy made the day seem so much more important. I did wonder what my parents might say about sharing Stanley but, since my parents weren't really shocked at anything I did, I was sure it would all work out. Everything usually does.

CHAPTER FIVE

Now, getting back to the case, we searched the park several times. We didn't come up with anything, other than a few gum wrappers and some shoelaces. We split up for a while; AJ took one side of the park and I took the other.

All I kept thinking was that, if we didn't solve our first case, we would never be famous and we might never get another case. Who in the world would hire two private detectives who couldn't even find missing sneakers?

All of a sudden, AJ came running toward me. "Come quick," he shouted, slightly out of breath.

"I hope it's good news," I said as I ran over to him.

"It's good news. We did it!"

I looked over toward the largest oak tree in the park and, wouldn't you know it, there were lots of sneakers all in a row. How did we miss that?

I was on top of the world. AJ was smiling and Stanley was jumping up and down.

We were on our way. I knew becoming a private detective would be a good thing. I even imagined that someday we might have a TV show or maybe even a Saturday morning cartoon. Now it was a definite possibility. I also knew I had found myself a good partner, even if he didn't like when I asked questions. I could live with that.

"Maybe we should leave the shoes here so we can find out who put them there," I said.

"Let's just hide behind the bushes and wait." We sat there for what seemed like forever, but it was only an hour or two. Then, all of a sudden, we saw a little puppy dog with a sneaker in his mouth. He walked over and put the sneaker down right next to the others.

"That's a new friend of mine," Stanley whispered to us. "It's Miss Bookmark's dog."

"Oh boy, now what?" I said. I began to think of how we were going to tell Miss Bookmark it was her dog. Well, the only thing to do was tell the truth. So AJ and I carried in a box with all the missing sneakers.

As soon as we walked in, Miss Bookmark seemed to sense our excitement. "I can tell by the smiles on your faces you two have some good news for me."

"Yes we do, Miss Bookmark. Emelina and I have found the sneakers." AJ said, not knowing how to tell her the bad news.

"You two should be very proud of yourselves," she said as she shook our hands.

"We are, but we have a small problem," I said.

Stanley came into the library with his new pal. Miss Bookmark smiled when she saw her dog.

"Winston, did you sneak off with the sneakers?" she asked, knowing the answer.

Winston put his little head down in a very cute but sad way. "Come over here," Miss Bookmark said, as she leaned down toward Winston and gave him a hug.

EXIT
Reference
SECTION
FRAGILE

"I think I know what happened," Miss Bookmark said. "Winston has been very lonely since the little boy next door moved away. He has been doing some very strange things."

She looked her dog in the eye and asked, "Do you promise never to do this again?"

Winston nodded yes.

Then, all of a sudden, Frankie Finkel walked into the library. "Any luck, Emelina?"

I handed Frankie Finkel his sneaker. "Boy, am I happy," Frankie said with a sigh of relief. "You saved the day. You're really good at this. I'll be sure to tell all my friends they can call you if they ever lose anything."

"Well, it wasn't only me," I said, pointing to my best buddies, Stanley and AJ. "We're a team."

"Thanks guys. You're a great team," Frankie said as he shook all of our hands. Miss Bookmark smiled at us and said, "You are very good detectives."

AJ and I looked at each other and smiled. Stanley winked at me, knowing that we would talk about it later.

I did realize that this case was just a bit more complicated than we thought but, when we finish Private Detective School in a couple of weeks, we will be more prepared for our next case. You will be hearing from us very soon and, I promise you, our next adventure will be lots of fun.

So, see you then....

About the Author

Marsha Casper Cook was born and raised in Chicago. She is a Partner of the World of Ink Network, Agent, Award-winning Script Writer, Novelist, Writing Coach, Media Release Specialist, Blog Talk Radio Host and Founder of Michigan Avenue Media. Marsha Casper Cook is the author of 10 published books and 11 feature-length screenplays, a literary agent with 15 years of experience and the host of BTR's World of Ink Network shows: A Good Story Is a Good Story and special editions of The World of Ink Network. She and her guests discuss writing and what's new in the entertainment field. Marsha has also appeared as a guest on other network shows and will continue to make frequent visits to other shows.

Soon to be released
Grand Central Station
A Romantic comedy about life love and family.

Visit Marsha's website at

www.MarshaCasperCook.com

Other children's books by Marsha Casper Cook:

The Busy Bus

The Magical Leaping Lizard Potion

I Wish I Was a Brownie

Snack Attack